# Promises, Promises

1. It is January the first, New Year's Day, so Pat doesn't have to deliver the post today. Julian is helping him to put up a new calendar on the kitchen wall.

2. Julian points to a space with NEW YEAR RESOLUTIONS written on it. "What's this for?" asks Julian. "What are New Year resolutions?"

3. "A resolution is a sort of promise," says Pat. "It's a tradition that people make them today, and try to keep them for the rest of the year."

4. "You mean something like you could promise to give me my pocket money on time?" says Julian. Pat laughs. "Something like that!"

5. "I'm going to make a resolution," says Julian, looking down at his muddy shoes. "I promise that I'll try to keep myself clean and tidy."

6. "Good for you!" says Pat. "I'm going to make a resolution, too. I promise to get up on time in the morning, EVERY morning."

7. "We'll see which of you keeps your resolution for the longest time," says Sara, handing Julian the shoe brush and some polish.

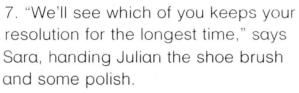

8. Pat writes the resolutions on the calendar. "It's my day off, so today doesn't count," says Pat. "We'll start from tomorrow."

9. Next morning Pat rushes down to the kitchen in a panic. He looks at the clock. "Oh, no, I forgot to set the alarm clock," he says. "I'm late!"

10. Sara comes into the kitchen. "Have you got time for a cup of tea?" she asks. Pat pulls on his jacket and grabs his cap. "No!" he says. "Come on, Jess!"

11. Julian get ups, makes his bed, puts his books on the shelves and tidies away his comics. He has a shower and makes sure the bathroom is clean and tidy.

12. "You look smart today," says Sara. "Thanks," says Julian. "I'm just going to brush these cat hairs off my coat, then I'm going to call for Charlie."

13. The snow is starting to melt but the garden path is still icy. Julian is so busy admiring his shiny shoes that he doesn't notice...

14. Whoops! Julian slips on the ice and lands in a patch of wet, sticky earth. His shoes and clothes are covered in soggy brown mud.

15. That night Pat comes home. "Well, how did YOU get on?" he asks, looking at Julian's muddy shoes. "Not very well, Dad," says Julian.

16. Pat and Julian look at the calendar. "My NEW New Year resolution," says Pat, "is not to make one!" Julian laughs. "Me, too, Dad!"

# New Arrivals

Pat was out delivering the post one spring morning. The birds were singing and green leaves were starting to cover the trees after a long, hard winter. Pat felt happy as he drove into the yard at Peter Fogg's farm. The farm was last on Pat's round, and he looked forward to having a chat with Peter – and perhaps a cup of tea. Peter was nowhere to be seen, but Pat knew he was around somewhere because his sheepdogs were in the yard, and they were never far from Peter's side.

"Hello, Peter!" called Pat.

Pat heard a voice from the barn. "Over here, Pat. In the barn."

Pat found Peter sitting on a straw bale with two tiny lambs in his arms. "New arrivals, eh, Peter?" said Pat.

Peter sighed. "A bit too new, Pat. Some of the lambs have come early. I wasn't expecting them to be born for a couple of weeks yet."

Pat looked concerned. "They'll be all right, though, won't they? You can keep them in here if it's too cold for them outside, can't you?"

"Yes, that's not a problem," said Peter. "What is a problem is that lots of the ewes have had twins, and a couple have had triplet lambs.  And they don't have enough milk to feed them." He held up the lambs in his arms. "These two are little orphans. I'll have to bottle feed them or they'll die.

They need feeding every few hours, day and night, so it's quite a job." Peter yawned. "I've been up all night with these two, and I think I'll have more to look after before the day's out."

Pat took off his cap and jacket. "You go and get yourself some breakfast and check on the ewes," he said. "I'll look after these two."

"Thanks, Pat," said Peter.

Peter was soon back with two more lambs that needed hand feeding.

Pat looked at his watch. "Look, I've got to get back to the post office," he said. "Mrs Goggins will be wondering where I am.  But I'll come back and help as soon as I can."

Pat was back at the farm within an hour, and this time he wasn't alone. Sara, Julian and Charlie were with him. They took one lamb each and Pat and Sara showed the boys how to feed the lambs.

Peter went off to have a couple of hours sleep, then he went to check on the flock. He came back with three more lambs in his arms. One of them was very tiny. Peter held it in his big hands. "This one will have to stay in the warm near the oven in the kitchen until it's bigger," he sighed. "I don't know where I'll find the time to look after him. It's great that you've been able to help, but you can't stay all the time." He pushed his cap back on his head. " I don't know what I'm going to do. I don't think I can cope on my own."

Soon all the lambs had been fed and lay sleeping on the straw. Peter was in the kitchen showing Julian how to take care of the tiniest lamb. They laid him in a cardboard box filled with soft rags and pushed the box against the oven of the big stove with the door open. "He'll need to be fed at least every two hours," said Peter, shaking his head.

Peter and Julian weren't the only ones who were busy. Pat left Sara and Charlie in the barn and set off towards the village.

He was back soon, and this time Ted Glen and Miss Hubbard were with him. When he had told them about Peter's problem they had agreed to help out right away.

Peter was very grateful. He didn't know what to say. "And that's not all," said Pat. "I've organised a sort of rota of helpers. I've pinned it up outside the church hall."

10

Lots of people have offered to help. They'll come out for a couple of hours each day so that you can get some sleep and look after the rest of the animals until the lambs can look after themselves."

Pat's rota worked very well. Every day some of the villagers went to the farm to help with the lambs. Peter still had to do most of the night feeds, but he didn't mind. The orphan lambs that might have died grew healthy and strong. As soon as they could look after themselves, Peter put them out in the fields that were now full of juicy green spring grass.

There was less and less work for the helpers to do, and soon Julian was the only one left. He had looked after the tiniest of the orphan lambs after school each day and now it, too, was fit and strong.

Soon the day came for the lamb to join the rest of the flock out in the fields. The weather was getting warmer now, and Peter told Julian that the lamb would do well.

Julian was pleased to see it running and gambolling about with the other lambs, but he felt sad in a way. He knew that lambs can't be treated like pets, but he had grown fond of the little orphan.

A few weeks later all the helpers went back to Peter's farm for one last time. They all met up in the barn. But they didn't go to feed the lambs. Peter had asked them all to a barn dance as his way of saying thank you. There were hay bales to sit on and Peter had hung strings of lights from the rafters. A friend of his played the fiddle and everyone joined in the dancing. When there was a break in the dancing the villagers opened the big barn doors to watch the lambs they had cared for leaping and running around the big meadow. They seemed to be having fun.

"What do you call a lamb leaping over a stile?" asked Julian.

Everyone laughed. They ALL knew that old joke!  "A little woolly jumper!" they all said at once.

# Lambs, Lambs and More Lambs

Pat took a picture of Peter's lambs. How many can you count? Look carefully – some of them have chosen good hiding places! How many sheepdogs can you count? Write your answers in the boxes at the bottom of the page.

lambs        sheepdogs

Check your answers on page 61.

12

# postman Pat™
## ANNUAL 1997

Written by Brenda Apsley
Illustrated by Ray and Christine Mutimer

POSTMAN PAT © Woodland Animations Limited 1996.
Licensed by Copyrights.

Published in Great Britain in 1996 by
World International Limited,
Deanway Technology Centre, Wilmslow Road, Handforth,
Cheshire SK9 3FB.

Printed in Italy.
ISBN 0 7498 2800 5

£5.50
UK only

# CONTENTS

# SPOT THE DIFFERENCES

Here are two pictures of the barn dance at Peter's farm. They may look the same, but there are 5 things that are different in the bottom picture. Draw rings around the 5 differences.

Check your answers on page 6l.

# Charlie Chalk.

# The Secret

1. Charlie has a secret. He has found out that it is Captain Mildred's birthday on Sunday, and he wants to plan a party for her. A surprise party.

2. Charlie wants to keep the party a secret, so he whispers the details to the others. That way Captain Mildred will not hear about it.

3. The first person Charlie meets is Edward who, as usual, has just woken up. "Can you keep a secret?" asks Charlie. "Of course I can," yawns Edward.

4. "We're having a surprise party on Sunday for Captain Mildred on the Buttercup," Charlie whispers. "Three o'clock. Pass it on."

5. Edward meets Lewis T Duck. "Surprise party on Monday for Captain Mildred on the Buttercup," Edward tells Lewis. "Three o'clock. Pass it on."

6. Lewis meets Mary the Hover fairy. "Surprise party on Monday for Captain Mildred. Bring butterflies," whispers Lewis. "Three o'clock. Pass it on."

7. Mary flies to Trader Jones's store. "Meat pies party on Monday for Captain Mildred. Bring butterflies," she says. "Three o'clock. Pass it on."

8. Arnold comes into Trader's store. "Meat pies party on Monday for Captain Mildred. Bring butterflies," says Trader. "Bring a mop. Pass it on."

15

9. Arnold meets Charlie. "Meat pies party on Monday for Captain Mildred. Bring butterflies," whispers Arnold. "Bring a mop. Put it on."

10. "Meat pies?" says Charlie. "A mop?  What are you talking about?" Arnold isn't really sure. "Er, I think it's some kind of party. A secret party."

11. The party! Charlie realises what has happened. No one has heard the message properly because they have all been whispering!

12. Charlie sends out invitations. He writes them out this time. Captain Mildred loves the secret birthday party. What a surprise!

# Charlie Chalk.
## The Coconut Race

Charlie Chalk and Trader Jones are having a race – a coconut race. They are going to see who is first to climb to the top of the coconut trees.

Play this game with a friend. One player can be Trader, the other

Charlie. You need a small counter each, and a coin. Take turns to flip the coin. If it lands on HEADS move your counter ONE ring up your tree. If your coin lands on TAILS, move up TWO rings. The first player to reach the top is the winner!

# Special Delivery

It was Saturday, and it was a very special day for the Pottage twins, Katy and Tom. It was their birthday, and Mrs Pottage had promised them an extra special party. They had invited all their friends from the village.

Sara and Julian were having breakfast in the kitchen. "What are you going to do today?" Sara asked Julian. "Anything interesting?"

Julian shook his head. "No, Charlie's gone to stay with his cousin for the weekend. I'll probably play on my computer or something."

"I'm going to be busy," said Sara. "I've offered to help Mrs Pottage with the twins' party. It's hard work organising everything on your own. There's all the food to get ready, the balloons to blow up, the party games and music to organise, the pass the parcel gifts to wrap. And the twins are sure to be into everything."

"I'll help too, if you like," said Julian. "It will give me something to do. I'll take Tom and Katy out into the garden and play with them while you and Mrs Pottage get everything ready. I could make up a few party games, too, if you like."

"What a good idea, Julian," said Sara. "That will be a real help. Thanks."

So later, while Sara and Mrs Pottage were busy in the kitchen, Julian took Katy and Tom into the garden. They played hide and seek, tag and statues, then it was time for the twins to have a bath and get changed into their best clothes.

That gave Julian lots of time to get his games organised before the guests started to arrive.

When the last of the guests had arrived and the gifts and cards had been opened, Julian brought out the first game. "It's called musical cushions," he said. "You play it just like musical chairs, but with cushions. I've brought a Happy Birthday tape to use for the music." The guests thought it was better fun than musical chairs, because they could jump on to the vacant cushions and roll about the floor! The winner was Tom Pottage, so everyone sang Happy Birthday to him at the end.

"The next game is like Pin the Tail on the Donkey," said Julian. "But instead of a tail, you have to pin a cap on the postman, Postman Pat!" Julian had drawn a big picture of Pat without his cap. He stuck it on the wall. The guests took turns to try to pin his cap in place. It was difficult because they had to do it wearing a blindfold. Pat's cap ended up in some very odd places! Katy Pottage pinned it to his shoe!

After that the guests all sat down to eat. There was jelly and trifle and sausage rolls and cheese cubes on sticks. Everyone had a paper hat to wear and a cracker to pull and they all laughed when they read the silly jokes out loud.

While the guests were finishing their tea, Julian asked his mum for the spare paper plates and went into the living room. Sara couldn't think what he was going to do with them.

She soon found out when Julian came back wearing a paper plate mask he had made. It looked just like Jess! The children all thought it was great, and wanted to know how he had made it, so Julian showed them. While they were all quiet Sara and Mrs Pottage cleared the food away.

stared. What could it be?

"Come on, aren't you going to open it?" asked Pat.

Katy pulled off the ribbon and opened the box. She gasped. "Oh, it's a cake!" she said.

"And it looks just like Jess!" said Tom.

Pat lit the candles on the cake and as the guests all sang Happy Birthday, Katy and Tom blew them all out and made a special wish.

What do you think they wished for? I think it was for a birthday party like this one every year!

Soon there was a tiger and a teddy bear, a rabbit and a fox at the party! Tom and Katy and their friends all had fun running around and making animal noises that matched their masks.

After playing some more games it was time for the guests to go home. But there was one more surprise for Tom and Katy before that...

There was a knock at the front door. Who could it be?

"Answer the door will you, Tom and Katy?" Mrs Pottage asked, winking at Julian and Sara.

Tom opened the door and there stood Postman Pat in his uniform with Jess by his side. "Special delivery for Katy and Tom Pottage," said Pat in his most official-sounding voice.

Pat handed over a big box with a large bow on top. Katy and Tom

"I was trying to make this old engine into a sort of big washing machine. I thought we could do with a laundry on Merrytwit. I got it going – but I think I put in too much soap."

"So this snow is really soap flakes?" asked Charlie.

Trader nodded. "It's not very good, is it?" he asked.

"It's not very good snow," said Charlie. "But I've got an idea. We can't have a snowball fight, so we'll have a soap fight instead! Come on!"

Charlie and the others were about to go outside when Captain Mildred handed each of them a mop from behind Trader's counter. "Not so fast," she said. "The soap fight can wait. Come with me because A, the Buttercup is covered in soap flakes and B, she needs a jolly good wash. Come on! Follow me!"

The others followed her, even Trader and Charlie. The soap fight would have to wait. You don't argue with Captain Mildred.

# Dawn and Dusk

1. Pat, Sara and Julian decide to go on some special walks with the wardens in the country park.

2. The first walk is a bird watching walk. It starts very early in the morning when the birds start singing.

3. Pat laughs as everyone yawns. Because he works as a postman he is used to being up so early!

4. The next walk starts very late at night, to look out for bats and owls and moths.

5. Pat has been up since early in the morning and feels very tired. He should be in bed by now.

6. Sara and Julian and the other walkers stop to listen for owls hooting. Moths fly near the torches.

7. "Where's Pat?" Sara whispers to Julian. They look around and shine their torches.

8. "There he is!" says Julian, pointing his torch at a big tree. Pat is leaning against the tree, fast asleep!

# Night and Day

Julian did a report on his morning and night walks at school. Can you help him to match the animals to their names by writing the names in the spaces?

hedgehog    fox
rabbit      deer
butterfly   badger
robin       squirrel

|  |  |  |  |
|---|---|---|---|

|  |  |  |  |
|---|---|---|---|

Julian made a night and day chart. Can you help him by drawing in little pictures of the animals that come out at night and those that come out in the day?

|  |  |
|---|---|
|  |  |

40

This picture shows some night animals. Count how many of each and write the numbers in the boxes at the bottom of the page.

The answers are on page 61.

**bat** [ ]

**moth** [ ]

**owl** [ ]

41

# A Special Day in Greendale

It was Friday morning and everyone seemed to be busy in Greendale. As Pat drove his van on his morning round to deliver the post he saw lots of people up and about, though it was still very early.

Pat met Miss Hubbard at her garden gate. She was going out as Pat was going in. Pat handed her an envelope.

"Nearly ready for the big day?" asked Pat.

"Nearly," said Miss Hubbard. "I just need some bits of black wool and it's almost finished. Granny Dryden is sure to have some."

"I'll let you get on then," said Pat as Miss Hubbard cycled off towards the village.

Pat's next call was at the vicarage. "I don't suppose you've got any black wire, have you, Pat?" asked the Reverend Timms.

"Sorry, Vicar," said Pat, handing over the post. "Why don't you see if Ted has some?"

"Good idea," said the vicar. "I have to go near his house to collect a red scarf anyway, so I'll call in," and he hurried off towards Ted's house.

At Granny Dryden's house Pat found a big sack of straw outside the door. "Shall I bring this in for you, Granny?" asked Pat.

42

"Yes please," said Granny Dryden. "I need it for the overalls. I've already got the cap. It's around here somewhere, I know it is."

"I must get on with my round, or I'd help you look for it," said Pat.

"Oh, no you won't," said Granny Dryden. "This is a secret even from you, Pat!"

Pat laughed. "OK, see you tomorrow then."

"Sounds interesting!" said Pat. "See you all tomorrow at the village hall."

Pat's last call was at the police station. He found PC Selby outside, just getting on his bike. "Nice day," said Pat.

Pat's next call on his round was at the Pottage house. "Everything ready for tomorrow?" Pat asked Tom and Katy.

"Yes, I found lots of cotton wool and a deerstalker cap," said Tom.

"And I borrowed a pair of long brown socks from Peter Fogg," said Katy.

"And I found this little toy dog in the toy box," said Mrs Pottage.

PC Selby waved to Pat and pedalled off. "Yes, Pat," he called over his shoulder. "Sorry I can't stop to talk, but I've got to get into Pencaster. The butcher is lending me a big white apron for tomorrow."

What are the villagers up to? Can you guess?

The next morning lots of cars and buses arrived in Greendale. Arrows pointed the way to the church hall. Sara was sitting at a table outside selling sheets of paper to the visitors. The villagers were having a Scarecrow Hunt to raise funds for repairs to the church. All the villagers had made a scarecrow that looked like someone in the village, and the visitors had to find them with the help of some clues on the sheet of paper and tick them off a list. There was going to be a prize for the visitor who found them all.

This wasn't as easy as it sounds because some of the scarecrows were in VERY odd places! Ted Glen had put his scarecrow of PC Selby on his roof, and Alf Thompson had put his scarecrow of Peter Fogg in a wheelbarrow in his front garden!

There was a special mini scarecrow hunt for the village children. Pat watched Julian and Charlie set off around the village, then he went inside the post office with a bag of straw under his arm. He was laughing to himself as he went in...

After an hour or so Julian and Charlie had ticked off nearly all the names on their list. They had found

44

the scarecrow of Mrs Goggins sitting on a bench in the park, and the one of Miss Hubbard on an old bike leaning against the wall outside the shop. There was even a scarecrow of Jess high up in a tree!

"Only two more to find now," said Julian.

Charlie looked over at the post office and pointed. "Look, over there!"

Julian smiled.

They walked over to the post office where a scarecrow of Postman Pat was leaning against the post box. Straw stuck out of the bottom of his trousers and sleeves, his glasses were on crooked, and his cap was on back to front.

Julian and Charlie laughed. "I think this is one of the best scarecrows of all, don't you?" asked Julian.

Charlie nodded. "Yes, it looks quite real," he said.

The boys moved closer to take a better look and jumped in the air when the scarecrow took their hands and winked at them!

Pat had decided to play a practical joke on them by dressing up as a scarecrow!

# WHICH SCARECROW?

Can you match up the things that go with each scarecrow? Write a number for each scarecrow.

Mrs Gogg

1

Ted Glen

2

3

Sam Waldron

4

Major Forbes

The answers are on page 61.

# Autumn

It was autumn in Greendale and Julian was back at school again after the long summer holiday. This term one of the topics his class were doing was recycling. They were learning all about not throwing things away that could be used again. Glass bottles can be melted down and made into more glass bottles, aluminium cans can be recycled, and old newspapers can be turned into new ones. It helps save the earth's supplies.

Julian was organising things at home so that anything that could be recycled was not thrown away. He had got some cardboard boxes from the supermarket and was recycling them as collecting boxes. Newspapers went in one box, and drinks cans in another. There was a box for old clothes, too. The good ones would go to a charity shop, and the scraps could be used as dusters. There were three separate boxes for glass: for brown, green and clear glass.

Pat was busy in the garden. Julian had told him how good kitchen waste was when it was turned into compost, so Pat had made a big compost heap and put waste like egg shells, potato peelings and tea leaves on it. When it rotted down it would make good soil for the garden and help Pat's fruit and vegetables to grow.

Pat looked into the garage as Julian was putting the last label on his recycling boxes. "That's great," said Pat. "It's a really good idea. When you've filled the boxes I'll give you a lift down to the bottle and paper banks in the supermarket car park in Pencaster."

Pat and Julian went outside again. Pat looked at the garden. "I wish I could organise the garden as well as you've organised the recycling boxes," he said. "That good weather we had has made everything ripen at once. The fruit bushes are full of berries and fruits. We won't be able to eat them all before they start to get too ripe. It seems a shame, but some will have to be thrown on to the compost heap if I can't find enough people who might like them. Trouble is, most people grow fruits and vegetables of their own."

Julian was putting some empty glass jam jars into his clear glass box when he had an idea.

He told Pat all about it and soon they were both busy in the kitchen...

Pat got out the cook books and found recipes for all kinds of jams and pickles and chutneys using the fruits and vegetables in the garden. They even found a way of adding fruits to vinegar to make them special for cooking.

It was hard work, but soon the kitchen was full of good smells as big pans bubbled and boiled on the cooker. And of course Julian had all sorts of clean glass jam jars and bottles to put them in.

When Sara came home she found the kitchen table covered in all sorts of good things.

But Julian hadn't finished yet. He went out to the garage and came back with some scrap paper and some bits of fabric that were left over from Sara's dressmaking. There were scraps of ribbon and lace, too.

Julian got out his scissors and coloured felt-tip pens. Soon he had cut out lots of labels and written what was in the jars on them. He glued them on the bottles and jars. Then he and Pat cut out circles of cloth and tied them to the jam jars with bits of ribbon and lace so that they looked like little hats.

"That's great," said Sara. "Really impressive. You two should go into business!"

Pat and Julian started to put the jars and bottles into the larder. "There's still too much stuff here for us," says Pat.

Julian has another good idea. "I know, we'll keep some and sell the rest at the autumn fair at church."

"Good idea!" said Pat. "Then we'll have recycled lots of stuff and raised some money for a good cause at the same time!"

# Music Makes

"Why not make some musical instruments using bits and pieces? It's a good way of recycling and having fun at the same time. I'll show you how."

## Rattle

Put a handful of rice in empty, washed cottage cheese tubs. Snap the lids back on and shake. Try filling them with other things to make different sounds. Try lentils, dried peas or small dried pasta shapes.

## Guitar

Find an old biscuit tin lid. Put four or five elastic bands on it, like guitar strings. Now strum the elastic strings.

## Trumpet

Ask a grown-up to make 4 little holes along one side of a kitchen roll tube. Cover one end with a piece of tissue paper held in place with an elastic band. Now blow gently into the other end. Cover different numbers of holes to make different sounds.

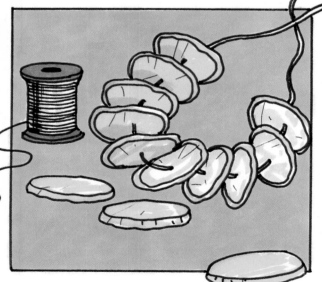

## Shaker

Collect lots of foil milk bottle tops and wash them. Ask a grown-up to thread them on to a length of cotton using a sewing needle. Tie the ends together and shake.

# Pantomime Time

1. This year the Greendale village pantomime is going to be Treasure Island. Auditions for parts are being held in the village hall.

2. Everyone acts out the person they would like to play. Pat is dressed up as Long John Silver and Julian is playing the part of Jim the cabin boy.

Sqwawk!

3. Pat wears a big hat and hops about on one leg. He has fun doing a silly pirate voice. "Ha-harrr, Jim lad!" he says. "Yo, ho, ho, and a bottle of rum!"

4. Charlie stands at the side of the stage and does the voice of the toy parrot pinned to Pat's shoulder. "Squawk!" he says. "Pieces of eight! Pieces of eight!"

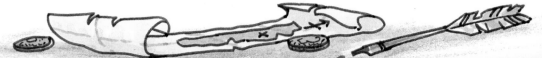

5. Sam Waldron and PC Selby make good pirates. They have a pretend fight with cardboard swords and Peter Fogg makes lots of noise when he is 'stabbed'!

6. Major Forbes has the right whiskers to play Squire Trelawney and Peter Fogg doesn't need a false beard to look like the pirate left on the island, Ben Gunn.

7. Soon everyone has had their turn. The Reverend Timms has chosen the cast. The villagers are all happy with the parts they have been given.

8. Miss Hubbard is going to paint the scenery. She is chatting to Pat about her ideas when she stops and points at the stage. "Look!" she says.

9. Pat and the others look at the stage. Jess is standing there with a pair of children's wellington boots on his front paws! He makes everyone laugh!

10. "What on earth has got into Jess, Pat?" asks the Reverend Timms. Jess walks around the stage. "What is Jess doing?" asks Julian.

11. "He's auditioning for a part in the pantomime," says Pat. "But there's no part for a cat in Treasure Island, Dad," says Julian.

12. Pat laughs. "I know," he says. "I think Jess is auditioning for the wrong pantomime. He wants to play Puss in Boots!"

# Pantomime Partners

1.

2.

3.

4.

5.

Can you match the people to the pantomimes? The picture clues will help.

Check your answers on page 61.

Mother Goose ☐

Jack and the Beanstalk ☐

Aladdin ☐

Snow White and the Seven Dwarfs ☐

Cinderella ☐

55

# Christmas Puzzle

It's Christmas morning. Give Pat, Sara and Julian their Christmas presents by following the lines.

Don't forget Jess.
There's a present for him too. Can you guess what their presents are?

The answers are on page 6l.

# CHRISTMAS WORD SEARCH

| l | m | c | k | a | z | r | a | t | s |
|---|---|---|---|---|---|---|---|---|---|
| c | r | a | c | k | e | r | n | r | s |
| j | e | r | b | y | n | c | d | e | s |
| n | i | d | j | k | o | i | h | e | t |
| g | n | i | k | c | o | t | s | g | h |
| m | d | h | a | l | l | n | q | u | g |
| e | e | i | o | x | l | e | t | v | i |
| b | e | o | p | w | a | f | v | w | l |
| f | r | c | p | q | b | e | l | l | t |
| g | e | k | a | c | d | r | u | s | x |

Can you find the 10 Christmas words in the word square? They are spelled out forwards, backwards, up and down, so you have to look carefully. The letters can be used more than once.

Tick off the words as you find them.

balloon
bell
cake
card
cracker

lights
reindeer
star
stocking
tree

The answers are on page 61.

# Christmas is Coming...

It would soon be Christmas, and everyone in Greendale was busy making things ready for the holiday. Coloured lights were hung all along the High Street, and Pat tied a tinsel star on the front of his Post Office van.

One afternoon after he had finished work, Pat helped Peter Fogg, Ted Glen and Alf Thompson to put up the tall Christmas tree that Sam Waldron had brought along in his mobile shop. It was going to stand in the square in the middle of the village so that everyone would see it. Pat stood on a tall ladder to decorate the tree with lights and lots of baubles.

The Reverend Timms was busy too, because he was planning a special Christmas carol concert for the children in the village hall, with a party afterwards.

Just as Pat had put the big shiny star right at the top of the Christmas tree and had climbed down the ladder, the vicar called him to one side.

"I have a favour to ask, Pat," he said, and he and Pat talked quietly for a few minutes, Pat nodding his head.

On the day of the carol concert Charlie called for Julian so that they could walk to the village hall together. "Ready, Dad?" said Julian.

"Er, no," said Pat. "I'm busy. Um, I don't think I'll be able to come to the concert this year. I've got...er...lots of presents to wrap. Yes, that's it, presents to wrap."

Julian was puzzled. "But you always come to the carol concert," he said. "Every year."

Pat always helped at the concert, moving chairs around and keeping the younger children happy. He enjoyed singing the carols, too.

Pat looked flustered. "Yes, I know, son, but, well, I just can't make it this year," said Pat.

Julian and Charlie went off to the concert and soon Pat was busy – but he wasn't only wrapping presents.

Pat took a big black bin bag from the cupboard under the stairs, put the gifts he had wrapped inside, and hurried off in the direction of the village hall...

Everyone enjoyed the carol concert and the party afterwards. When the last mince pie had been eaten and the last balloon had been burst and the last cracker had been pulled, the Reverend Timms called for everyone to be quiet.

A hush slowly fell over the room as all the children listened hard. "Shhh!" whispered the Reverend Timms. "I think I can hear something! Can you?"

"I can!" cried Katy Pottage. "I can hear bells."

"They must be the bells on Father Christmas's sleigh!" said Tom.

"Father Christmas is coming!" said Julian and Charlie together.

They were right. The bells got louder and louder and soon Father Christmas came into the hall with his big sack of presents. He sat down and the children all lined up to get their presents.

Julian was the last to collect his gift. The sack was almost empty now, and Father Christmas had to reach right down to the bottom to find the last parcel.

Julian stared at the sack in surprise. It seemed to be moving!

A furry little black head popped out of the sack. A furry little black head with pointed ears! It was Jess!

The others didn't notice because they were so busy opening their presents.

Julian gasped. "It's ..." he started to say.

But 'Father Christmas' put his fingers to his lips and winked. "Shhh," said Pat, and gently pushed Jess back into the sack out of sight. "I'm just helping out because the real Father Christmas is too busy wrapping presents. It had better be our secret, eh?"

Julian nodded. "Happy Christmas!" he said.

| l | m | c | k | a | z | r | a | t | s |
|---|---|---|---|---|---|---|---|---|---|
| c | r | a | c | k | e | r | n | r | s |
| j | e | r | b | y | n | c | d | e | s |
| n | i | d | j | k | o | i | h | e | t |
| g | n | i | k | c | o | t | s | g | h |
| m | d | h | a | l | l | n | q | u | g |
| e | e | i | o | x | l | e | t | v | i |
| b | e | o | p | w | a | f | v | w | l |
| f | r | c | p | q | b | e | l | l | t |
| g | e | k | a | c | d | r | u | s | x |

61